For Harry, L.G.
For Nicholas and Ned, S.G.

little bee books

An imprint of Bonnier Publishing Group
853 Broadway, New York, New York 10003
Copyright © 2008 by Lynne Garner.
Illustrations copyright © 2008 by Sarah Gill.
First published in Great Britain by Piccadilly Press.
This little bee books edition, 2015.
All rights reserved, including the right of reproduction
in whole or in part in any form.
LITTLE BEE BOOKS is a trademark of Bonnier Publishing Group,
and associated colophon is a trademark of Bonnier Publishing Group.
Manufactured in China 0715024
First Edition 2 4 6 8 10 9 7 5 3 1
Library of Congress Control Number: 2015934160
ISBN 978-1-4998-0135-4

www.littlebeebooks.com
www.bonnierpublishing.com

The Best Sweater

little bee books

by Lynne Garner
illustrated by Sarah Gill

It was Spindle's birthday. He was very excited as he opened his presents. Finally, there was only one present left.

Spindle ripped off the paper
to find a bundle of colors.
It was a sweater—the
BEST sweater he had
ever seen!

"Thank you,
Grandma,"
he said, putting it on.
"It fits perfectly!"

After breakfast, Spindle
and his brother and sister
sailed his new boat on the pond.

Spindle's warm, snuggly
sweater kept out the cold.

Spindle LOVED wearing his sweater.

He wore it *all* the time.

And even when it was too hot to wear, he always took it with him . . . just in case.

One windy day, Spindle
decided to fly his kite.
The kite danced up and down, around and around,
just like a leaf.

Suddenly, a huge gust of wind blew it high up into the trees, where it got STUCK.

Spindle clambered up the
branches. But as he stretched
out his arm to reach the kite . . .

he tore his
sweater!

RIP!
RIP!

Spindle ran home.
"Mama, there's a hole
in my best sweater!"
he cried.

"Don't worry, dear,"
Mama said as she sewed
it for him.

Sometimes, Mama insisted on washing Spindle's sweater.
It always smelled a bit funny the next day.

But it soon got
back to normal.

As time went by,
Spindle found he had
to pull REALLY hard to get
his sweater on.

Then one day, Spindle
pulled really, REALLY hard,
and it still wouldn't go over his ears!

"My sweater's shrunk!" he told Mama.
"No, it's you who are growing, dear,"
said Mama as she made two little cuts in
the neck so it would fit again.

One night, when Spindle was staying
at Grandma's house, there was a big storm.
The thunder crashed and the lightning flashed.
Poor Spindle was very scared, but he
didn't want to wake Grandma.
So he cuddled his sweater instead.

In the morning, Spindle's
grandma said,
"Spindle, dear, that sweater is
just too small for you now."

"No it's not," said Spindle,
trying to pull it over his tummy.

But he let Grandma
add some material
to the bottom and
the sleeves.

When Grandma came to visit again,
she brought Spindle a big present.

IT WAS
ANOTHER
SWEATER!

When Spindle put it on,
he found that the sleeves
were a little too long,

the neck was
a little too big,

and the waist was
a little too large.

"You can grow into this one," said Grandma, smiling.
"It's lovely, thank you," said Spindle, kissing his
grandma. "It's almost as nice as my BEST sweater."

When Spindle went out to play,
he wore his new sweater.
But he took his BEST sweater with
him . . . just in case.

That evening, when Spindle was asleep,
Grandma was very busy with his old sweater. . . .

The next day, Grandma had another surprise for Spindle.
She held up a brightly colored toy.
It was a RABBIT!
"I made it from your old sweater,"
she told him.

"Thank you," said Spindle.
"It's the BEST rabbit
in the world!"

And he took it with him
EVERYWHERE!